FLIGHT of the GRIZZLY

Fabian Grégoire

FLIGHT
of the
GRIZZLY

FIREFLY BOOKS

A FIREFLY BOOK

Published by Firefly Books Ltd. 2017

First printing

Publisher Cataloging-in-Publication Data (U.S.)

Library of Congress Cataloging-in-Publication Data is available

Library and Archives Canada Cataloguing in Publication

Grégoire, Fabian, 1975-
[Vol du grizzly. English]
     Flight of the grizzly / Fabian Grégoire.
Translation of: Le vol du grizzly.
Includes bibliographical references.
ISBN 978-1-77085-996-8 (hardcover)
     I. Title. II. Title: Vol du grizzly. English.
PZ7.G8623Fl 2017   j843'.914   C2017-902127-3

Published in the United States by
Firefly Books (U.S.) Inc.
P.O. Box 1338, Ellicott Station
Buffalo, New York 14205

Published in Canada by
Firefly Books Ltd.
50 Staples Avenue, Unit 1
Richmond Hill, Ontario L4B 0A7

Translator: Claudine Mersereau

Printed in China

Canada

We acknowledge the financial support
of the Government of Canada

Thanks to Marie Barguirdjian and Jean-Philippe Tastet
for opening Canada's doors, and their home, to me.
Thanks to Amie Enns, for the information about the
wildlife of British Columbia and the 60s music.

For the Indigenous peoples on Canada's west coast,
the thunderbird is one of the most powerful spirits —
a fantastic creature whose flapping wings make clouds roar
and whose blinking eyes light up stormy skies.
According to numerous legends, it can carry a whale in its talons
and then devour it at the top of a mountain.

However, it wasn't a thunderbird that was breaking the silence that day, and it wasn't a thunderbird that was tracing a trail of fire in the sky. It was a machine that was disturbing the calm of this wild land. And for the three occupants of the plane in distress, the situation didn't have much in common with the poetry of an Indigenous tale.

"Mayday! Mayday! Goose CF-RQI here. Right motor on fire. I'm going to perform an emergency water landing south of Petrel Channel …"

Despite the circumstances, everyone was calm onboard the plane. My father already had 18 years experience as a bush pilot, and my friend George usually kept a cool head no matter what happened. As for me, I had been born aboard a seaplane 11 years earlier. It took a lot for the three of us to lose our cool!

"George! Buckle up for landing … "
"Right away, sir!"

Dad had just put out the fire with the engine's fire extinguisher, and so it was with a stopped propeller that we found ourselves on this isolated channel.
"Jessie, prepare the rope! We're going to try to tie ourselves to the rocks over there."

The Goose calmly glided in, just with its momentum. Once the second propeller had stopped, I was able to get out through the cockpit window and slide along the nose of the plane. In one leap, I landed on shore and tied the rope to an old tree trunk.

I know seaplanes well! At Raincoast Airlines base camp, I often fill the planes' gas tanks, and sometimes I warm up the motors before takeoff.

"I'll be here for a while," Dad said. "I'm going to put out a radio call so someone will come get you."

That's how we do it here: when travelers are having trouble or there's an emergency, the closest plane changes route to come to the rescue.

George and I had an exam the next day at Ocean Falls, for correspondence school. From my point of view, there was nothing urgent about the situation, but …

Just like that, five minutes later, our rescue was organized.
"Ned's going to come get us. He's near Prince Rupert. He'll be here in
about an hour."

Ned was Dad's pilot colleague. Together, they had created Raincoast Airlines, a
small airline company like 10 others in British Columbia. Business was going well.
The company's fleet included three types of seaplanes: the Grumman Goose, the
Noorduyn Norseman and the de Havilland Beaver.

"Well, I'm going to look at it more closely. Go walk around while we wait for
Ned," Dad yelled out.

So George and I went to explore the surroundings, first because Dad hates it when we watch him when he has his face in a motor, but mostly because we could see abandoned totem poles rising out of the greenery not far from us. George was dying to get a closer look at them.

"Did your people carve these?" I asked him.

"I'm not too sure … I'm not an expert," he answered.

George is a member of the Kwakwaka'wakw people, one of the many Indigenous communities who've lived on this coast for thousands of years. We Europeans only arrived in this region 300 years ago.

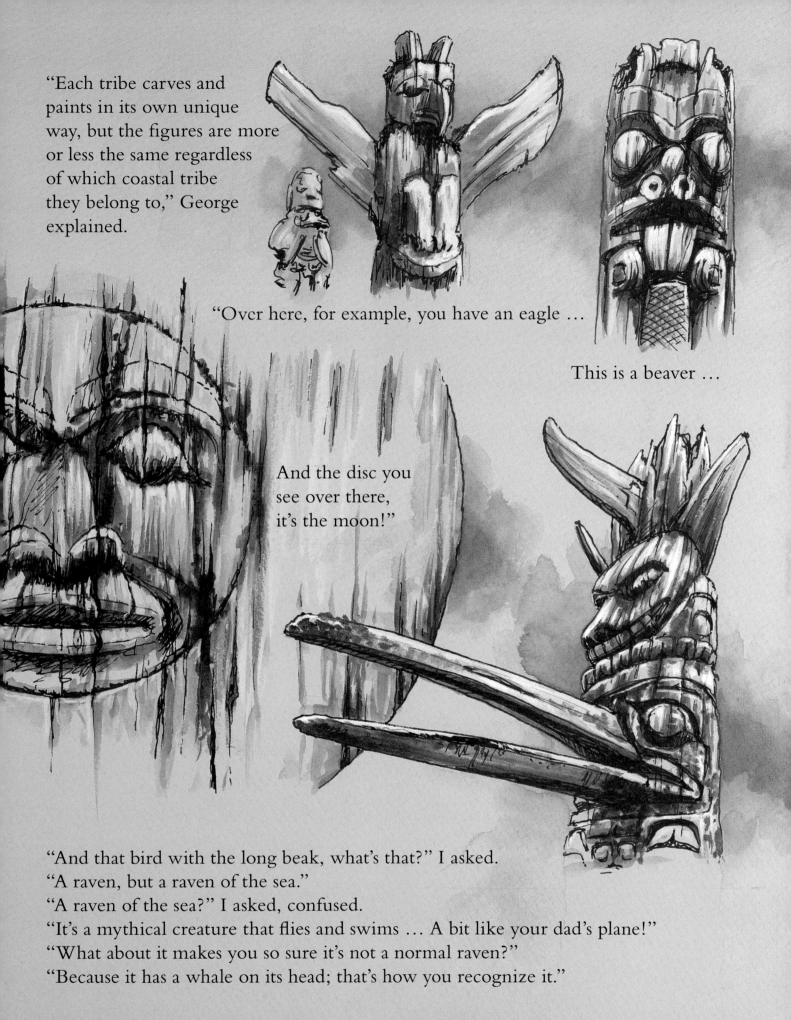

"Each tribe carves and paints in its own unique way, but the figures are more or less the same regardless of which coastal tribe they belong to," George explained.

"Over here, for example, you have an eagle …

This is a beaver …

And the disc you see over there, it's the moon!"

"And that bird with the long beak, what's that?" I asked.
"A raven, but a raven of the sea."
"A raven of the sea?" I asked, confused.
"It's a mythical creature that flies and swims … A bit like your dad's plane!"
"What about it makes you so sure it's not a normal raven?"
"Because it has a whale on its head; that's how you recognize it."

That's the day George told me all about the real and mythical animals that populate his people's legends. Until then, I hadn't paid much attention to Indigenous art. But all of a sudden, thanks to my friend, all of these incredible creatures seemed to come alive around us.

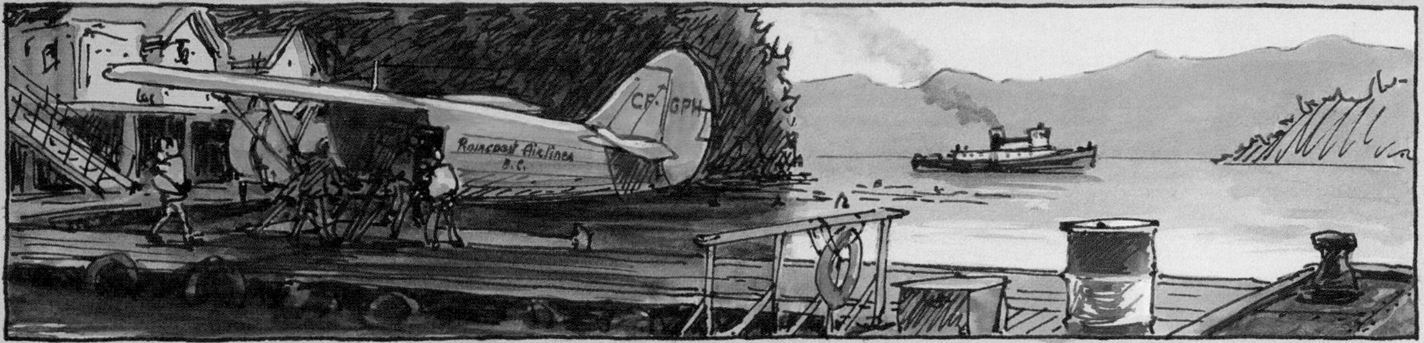
CF-GPH
Raincoast Airlines
B.C.

At that very moment, 100 miles from us, Ned and his passengers were boarding a Norseman. I was told this part of the story later, but for you to understand, it's best that I tell you now …

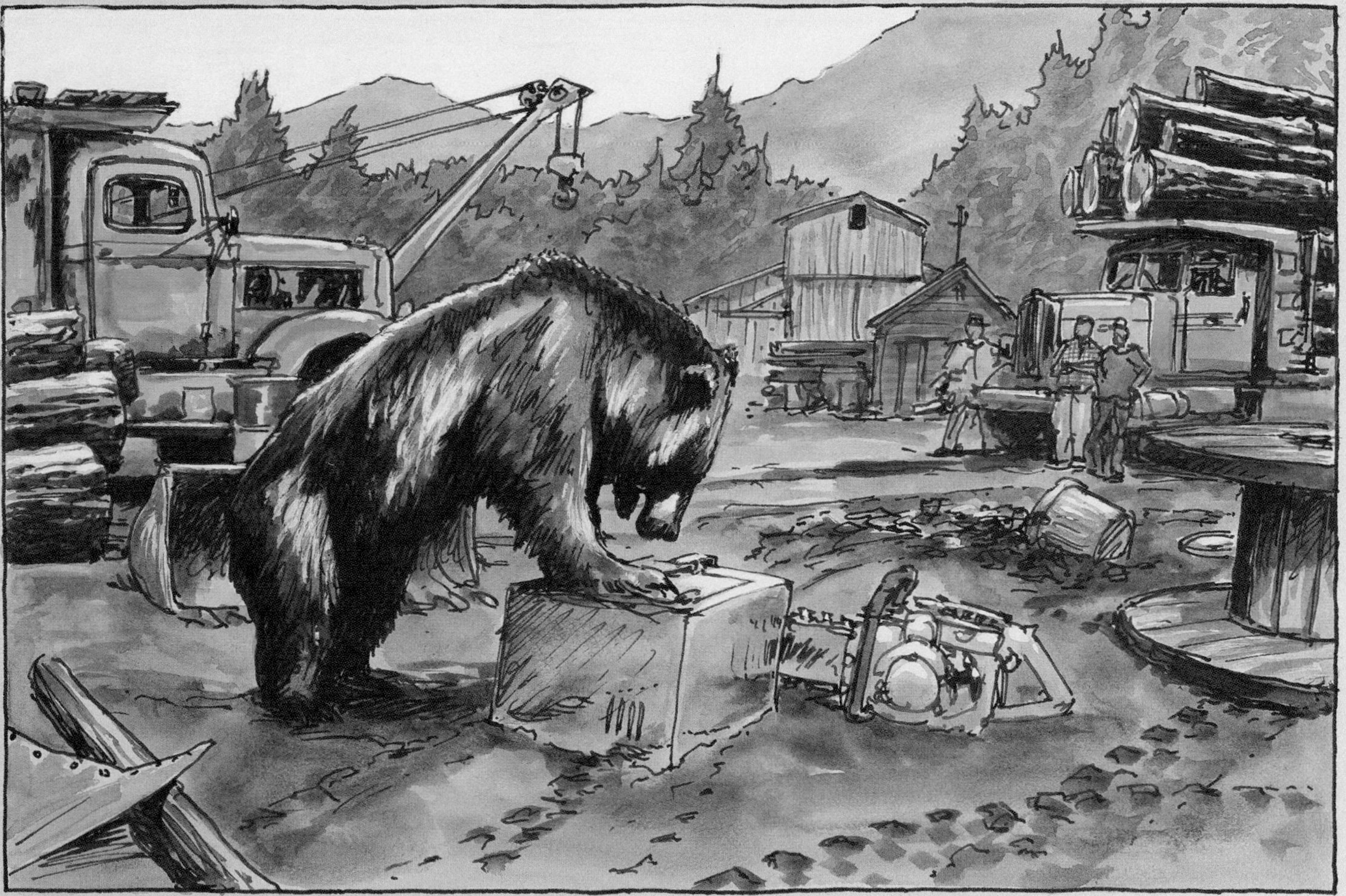

At the time, loggers at a camp set up at Union Inlet were dealing with an aggressive grizzly. He would approach the men and steal their provisions. Since the camp's boss was a skilled businessman, he had managed to sell the animal to the director of a zoo in the United States, but now the bear needed to be captured.

That morning, the loggers had managed to capture the grizzly with the help of a trap. With a dart filled with a powerful sedative, the zoo's director had tranquilized the animal in preparation for its flight south.

After a few tries, the men had managed to load the beast into Ned's plane.

"It's a young male. He must be over 400 pounds!"

"How much time do we have before he wakes up?"

"A good three hours!" answered the zoo director.

"So let's not waste any time … We're taking off right away!" the pilot had decided.

Meanwhile, George and I had made our way toward what was left of an Indigenous home.
"I have to pee … Wait for me, okay?" I said.
"What?" George answered.

George seemed lost in his thoughts. With his fingertips, he was brushing the half-rotten cedarwood that was covered with moss. Leaving my friend with his thoughts, I pressed into the bushes to do what I had to do.

In the middle of the channel that spread out in front of us, a pod of killer whales was slowly swimming upstream. Their calls managed to shake George out of his dreams ...
"Jess! Come see this! There are orcas … Oh, Jess! Where are you?"

"Jess?"
Only silence answered George's calls.

"Grraaarrr!"   "Aaaahhhhh!"   "Ha, ha! I got you good!"

"You crazy or what? I almost had a heart attack … "
"Don't exaggerate! He's got a scary face, sure, but it's nothing to faint over!"
"You obviously don't know who this is! It's a mask that represents Bukwus. Where did you find it?"
"Over there, in the grass. What is it exactly, your Bukwus?"

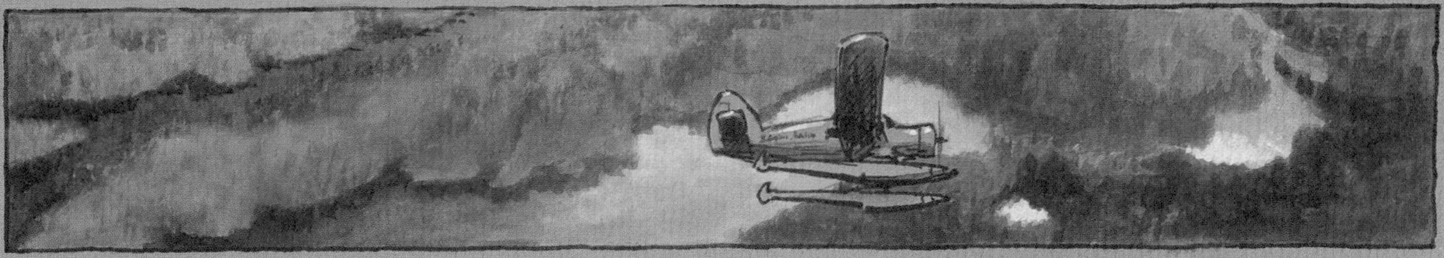

"It's the ghost of a drowned person … A very evil spirit that roams the forests. We also call him Man of the Sea," George explained, as we continued our stroll.

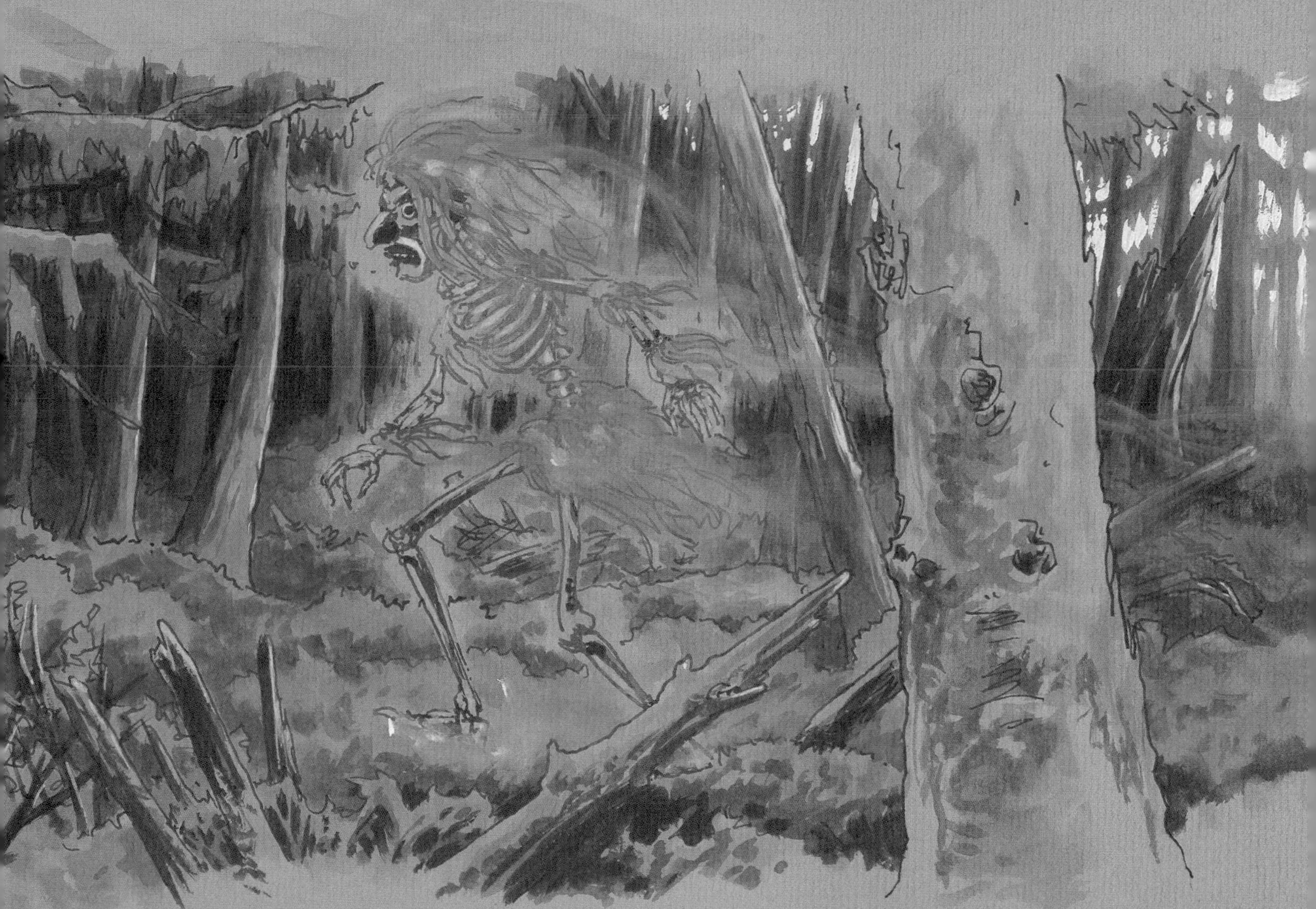

"You don't believe in this nonsense, do you?" I asked.
"Don't make fun, Jess … You whites are afraid of spiders and snakes, but you laugh when we talk to you about the King of Ghosts."
"So you've crossed path with Bukwus, have you?"
"I don't need to cross its path! It's enough to sense its presence and to see its tracks in the forest. When you see one of its victims, you'll understand what I mean."

I was going to start laughing when George put his hand on my arm to stop me from walking.

"Jessie … !"

In front of us, at the foot of a rocky hill, a strange clump of moss caught our eye.

"Is that … ?"

"Yes, Jess! We're in a cemetery."

I wasn't in the mood for jokes anymore. A gentle rain had started falling, and the surroundings had quickly taken on a very sinister air.

In the distance we could hear the sound of a purring motor.
"Ned must be arriving. We'd better go … "

We both took a few steps back, as if to avoid turning our backs to the skull that seemed to be watching us with its empty eye sockets. We hurried our way toward the Goose.

I even turned around two or three times to check that no evil spirits were following us. This fear wasn't going to leave me for the rest of the day. Had the spirit of Bukwus just played a trick on me?

Ned had tied his seaplane facing the shore, not far from where Dad's was.

"What's that thing you're transporting?" I asked him while getting into the copilot seat next to Ned.
"A grizzly, miss!" answered the man with the orange vest.
"No joke, a grizzly bear on a plane? And you're sure that … "
"We sedated him, Jessie!" Ned assured me, patting me on the back.
"Okay! I didn't say anything."

George loaded our bags into the Norseman and sat down beside the zoo director in the back. Ned started up his motor right away. He brought his seaplane to the middle of the channel, nose to the wind, and increased the throttle to full power. We were once again on our way to Ocean Falls.

"GGGRRRRHHH!"

Spread out on the floor of the cabin and wrapped up in a net, the grizzly was letting out deep grunts.

"He's not completely asleep … " George had whispered to me while boarding the plane.

I turned around to look at George. The look of concern on his face did little to reassure me. All those stories of skulls and Bukwus were messing with my head! I had a hard time convincing myself there wasn't any danger.

Small islands and channels passed slowly under our floaters, and the Norseman's motor was running like clockwork. Everything seemed to be going well. However, the more time passed, the more frequently the grizzly grunted. Soon, the bear's paws started to flail around, but it was only after seeing the zoo director's pale face that I understood there was a problem!

Besides the pilot, I was the only person in the plane who was wearing a headset. Gripping Ned's sleeve, I told him in a low voice over the receiver:

"Ned! Look at the face the zoo director's making … Something isn't right with the grizzly."

Ned turned around toward the passengers. The zoo director was staring at the dark mass that was moving, more and more, on the floor of the cabin.
"Say, are you sure you injected your beast with the right dose?" shouted Ned.
"Ah … yeah, I think so," he replied.

"Can you give him another injection?"
"Well, I used up all my stock; I've got nothing left," the zoo director said sheepishly, hanging his head and staring at his feet.
"For goodness' sake! You're crazy, my man! Do you understand the situation you've put us in?"

Behind us, the grizzly was starting to struggle.

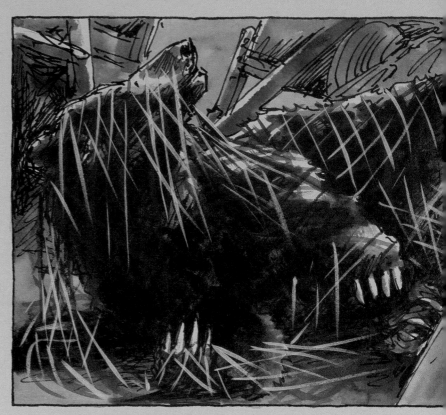

"There's nowhere to land around here!" grumbled Ned. "If I had known, I would have taken a different route … "

He grabbed the radio mic and put out a distress call: "This is CF-GPH in the northern part of Mount Parry. We have technical problems on board. I'm looking to make an emergency landing, over!"

Two emergency landings in one day … It was starting to be a bit much.

The bear started growling as it tried to free itself from the netting. "Ned!"

"Keep calm, Jess! There's water straight ahead. Everybody, get ready to get out as soon as we've stopped!"

George undid his seat belt and went to stand against the back panel of the cabin, next to one of the doors. His hand was on the handle, his eyes staring straight at the bear.

Huddled on his seat, the zoo director was trembling with fear.

The usual impact of the floaters hitting the waves let me know that we had touched down. Ned cut the gas and the Norseman started to slow down.

At that very moment, the grizzly managed to free itself from the net and rose up on its hind legs. There wasn't a second to waste!

"Run!" screamed Ned, untying his seat belt. He opened the door on his side of the cabin and jumped into the water head first.

As for me, I was so frightened by the bear's growls that I couldn't manage to unlatch my door. I'm not sure why, but my window had opened during landing. I fled the cockpit by scaling my seat and gripping the roof of the plane.

With its motors cut, the Norseman was drifting slowly toward the bank. George had been the first to jump out of the cabin, while the propeller was still turning. I saw that he was swimming toward the shore, about 50 feet from us. Ned was thigh deep in water and running, for better or worse, to distance himself from the plane. As for the zoo director, he was the last to jump, screaming in terror, and the grizzly was right on his heels!

Things happened so fast after this that my memory is a bit blurry. I remember that the bear leaped out of the cabin.

The ice-cold water definitely woke him up, and he seemed absolutely furious about the trick that had been played on him!

Perched on the wing of the Norseman, I was away from danger, but I also had a front row seat if the two men were caught by the bear and torn to shreds.

How could I help them? The radio! I suddenly thought. I went back into the cockpit and, fearing the bear might decide to come back, I started by carefully closing all of the doors on the seaplane.

In the meantime, the grizzly had almost caught up to the two men. To escape its claws, they had climbed the trunk of a birch tree. In their panic, they'd forgotten that bears are very good at climbing trees!

From then on, the only thing the two fugitives could count on was me.

I put on the headset and adjusted the radio frequency. I realized right away that it was useless: by the time help arrived, it would be too late.

Mouth wide open, the bear was advancing up toward the zoo director. I was starting to have trouble thinking.

Scare it! I had to find a way to scare it away!

There weren't a lot of options. Only a loud noise would make the animal flee.

I shifted the controls on the instrument panel and started the motor. It was still hot and started right away. Then I pushed on the gas lever while directing the plane, my feet on the rudder. I turned to look at the grizzly. It hadn't reacted, so I increased the power.

At that moment, the Norseman's right float touched a mud bank. The jolt hurled me to the left and made me let go of the controls. My head hit the door frame.

While I was massaging my temples and dizzy from the shock, I didn't notice that the plane was taking on speed. By the time I realized it, it was already too late.

Without really knowing why, my instinct was to fasten my seat belt. That must be what they call a survival instinct!

Thrown out of control on the waves, the Norseman made a sudden sharp turn …

It tipped and the end of its left wing touched the water …

There was another jolt and the Norseman turned around and tipped onto its other side …

Then it violently rammed into the shore.

When it was finally silent again I opened my eyes and saw nothing but branches and water in front of me. The plane had nose-dived and I was suspended from my seat, held only by my seat belt.

A minute or so later, Ned arrived, running.
"Jess! Are you okay?"
"I hurt everywhere, but it could be worse … What about the grizzly?"
"Gone, thanks to you …"

Frightened by the racket, the bear had run off into the forest. It wouldn't live out its life in a zoo after all.

George arrived shortly after and gave me a big hug.

"You scared me half to death, Jessie … "

"I know. It's a habit of mine," I whispered in his ear. I'm not sure if we were laughing or crying. Maybe a bit of both …

It was only when I turned around that I really understood what I had done. The Norseman's nose was crushed into the shore, its wings were embedded into tree trunks and the propeller blades were mangled. It was obvious the aircraft was broken beyond repair.

"I'm sorry about your plane … " I stuttered to Ned.

"I can replace a plane, Jess. We all got out of it alive; that's what's most important!"
The onboard radio was still working, so we were able to call for help.

A Beaver arrived from Bella Coola 40 minutes after our call. While we were boarding, George whispered, "I hope we're going to stay up in the air this time!"
I smiled back at him. Exhausted from the day, I quickly dozed off on his shoulder. We left the foot of Mount Parry, relieved, leaving the wreckage of the seaplane behind.

Many years later, we returned together to the site of the accident.
The remains of the Norseman were still there.

"Each civilization leaves a trace of its passage, Jess. For my people, it's totem poles.
For yours, it's wrecks," he said with a smile.
We wandered around the beach for a bit before returning to Port Hardy aboard the
small plane that I had just bought.

The design painted on the fin was created by George. I can explain what it represents, but now that you know this story, I think you can guess for yourself …

Since that day in 1967, I've never again made an emergency landing. Maybe it's George's design that's protecting me, or maybe Bukwus frightened me enough for a lifetime and decided to leave me alone. Maybe it's the benevolent spirit of the grizzly watching over me, as thanks for his freedom.

Who knows?

© Photo: Philippe Henry

THE GRIZZLY

Common in North America and in eastern Russia, the grizzly is a subspecies of the brown bear. Its global population is estimated to be over 200,000, of which approximately 25,000 live in Canada, many of them in British Columbia. An excellent salmon fisher, hunter and occasional scavenger (its strength allows it to steal prey that's already dead from other predators), it is omnivorous and feeds mainly on vegetation, such as roots, plants and berries.

Grizzly bears are massive animals. On four feet, they are "only" about 4-5 feet (1.2–1.5 m) tall, but standing on their rear legs, they reach 7 feet (2.1 m) or more. They weigh anywhere from 150 to 350 pounds (70–160 kg). The grizzly bear has a reputation for being aggressive and unpredictable, which may explain why 19th-century naturalists gave it the scientific name *Ursus arctos horribilis* (the horrible bear). It's true that grizzly attacks are reported every year in Canada and the United States, but these are often due to human negligence. Bears will attack if a person approaches prey that it's eating, if someone enters into its territory (usually around 60 square miles/155 km², which it might try to defend) or if someone approaches a female and her cubs. Generally however, the animal chooses flight rather than fight. Noise might ward off a bear, which is why people are advised to make themselves heard if they are in bear territory.

Indigenous people see the grizzly as a symbol of strength, a brother to humans (due to its ability to stand up on its hind legs) and a symbol of family loyalty (because bears fiercely defend their young).

In Canada, about 200 grizzly bears are killed every year by hunters, often illegally or for trophies. Today, British Columbia's Indigenous communities are fighting to stop trophy hunting of bears, where the hunters claim only the fur, head and paws, which are destined for "decorative" purposes or to be sold for its unproven medicinal benefits. This practice goes specifically against the Indigenous practice of always using the meat of any animal they kill.

To see a film about the grizzly bear visit http://www.bearsforever.ca/

Sketch of a **pts'aan or totem pole of the Nisga'a people** exhibited at the Quai Branly Museum in Paris. It represents the myth of Peesunt: a young girl is taken away by bears and gives birth to twins who are half man, half bear. The main figure at the bottom is the mother bear, which is an emblem of the clan. The top of the pole is occupied by a grizzly.

Footprints of a grizzly bear.

INDIGENOUS ART

The northwest coast of North America has been inhabited for thousands of years by Indigenous peoples who have developed an art form specific to the region. The styles generally differ from one tribe to the next, but the themes, figures and techniques have a common origin. Indigenous art from this coast offers two-dimensional painted designs and three-dimensional engravings and sculptures.

Designs are often painted on everyday objects, such as boxes, bowls, clothing and canoes. The base colors are black and red, often with a complement of blue-green. Certain tribes — in particular the Kwakwaka'wakw — also use yellow ocher.

These designs often represent animals, real or mythical, such as the thunderbird and the raven of the sea, discussed by Jessie in this book. Humans are also represented, but they are often associated with an animal; the concept of human-animal and animal-human transformation is common in Indigenous legends and spirituality. The visual codes used to symbolize a particular animal are not always easy to recognize. Thus, the head of the whale on the totem on page 13 looks more like the head of a wolf, but we can recognize it as being a whale because of the trademark small dorsal fin.

Among the creatures sculpted by Indigenous peoples, the totem poles leave the most lasting impression. These pillars carved out of cedar trunks often measure more than 65 feet (20 m) in height — a few are even close to 130 feet (40 m)! The figures sculpted into the wood are the same as those we find as painted sculptures. They usually tell the story of a clan or family, displaying the rank of the chief, outlining the clan's lineage, demonstrating its power. The totem pole is considered to be a member of the family, so it should be respected. You must never lean or sit on a totem pole, nor try to climb it.

In the 1960s, Indigenous art experienced a revival after a period of neglect. Today, in addition to many Indigenous artists on the northwest coast, and elsewhere in Canada, making traditional carved items, there are artists in coastal communities who are at the heart of contemporary creations, such as screen-printing, graphic design, jewelry making and computer graphics and design.

To learn more about Vancouver's Museum of Anthropology, visit http://moa.ubc.ca/

Painted pillars that supported a house.

A ceremonial mask representing a wolf.

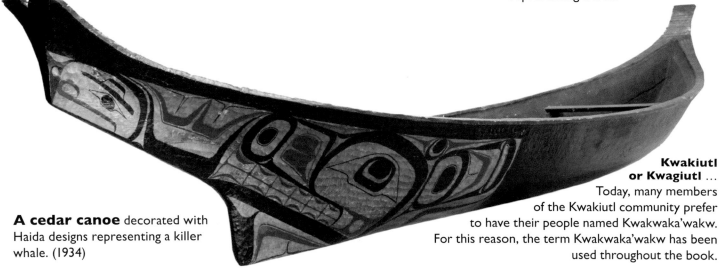

A cedar canoe decorated with Haida designs representing a killer whale. (1934)

Kwakiutl or Kwagiutl ...
Today, many members of the Kwakiutl community prefer to have their people named Kwakwaka'wakw. For this reason, the term Kwakwaka'wakw has been used throughout the book.

Part of a **Haida totem pole** sculpted around 1870, preserved in four parts after it fell in 1954. The piece on the left represents a bear, the one in the middle probably represents a man-cormorant and the one on the right is an eagle that is missing its beak.

© Photos: Fabian Grégoire, taken at the MOA (Museum of Anthropology in Vancouver).

Sculptures with flat graphic designs.

Painted totems poles installed in Stanley Park in Vancouver. The one on the right represents, from top to bottom, the moon face of a thunderbird, a mountain goat, and a grizzly holding a seal in its claws. It is a reproduction carved in 1964.

© Photos: Fabian Grégoire, taken at the MOA (Museum of Anthropology in Vancouver).

A human figure in three dimensions, carved into the pillar of a Kwakwaka'wakw home. (1906)

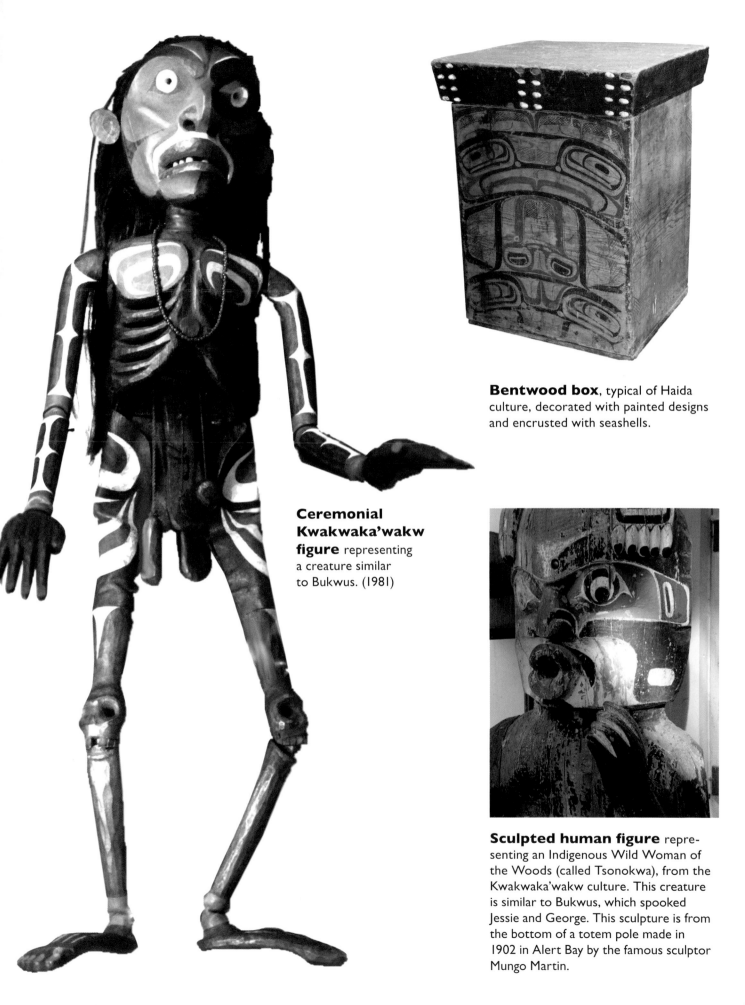

Ceremonial Kwakwaka'wakw figure representing a creature similar to Bukwus. (1981)

Bentwood box, typical of Haida culture, decorated with painted designs and encrusted with seashells.

Sculpted human figure representing an Indigenous Wild Woman of the Woods (called Tsonokwa), from the Kwakwaka'wakw culture. This creature is similar to Bukwus, which spooked Jessie and George. This sculpture is from the bottom of a totem pole made in 1902 in Alert Bay by the famous sculptor Mungo Martin.

THE SEAPLANE: A SYMBOL OF BRITISH COLUMBIA

British Columbia — the westernmost province of Canada, bordered by the Pacific Ocean — is a wild territory with a border that extends into islands and fjords for almost 1,000 miles (1,600 km).

The region's harsh terrain, wild environment and sparse population limited the development of a road network. Marine transportation through the many inlets and bays is slow and impractical, so the fast and easily maneuvered seaplane (also called a floatplane) became the preferred mode of transportation. Among the air carriers, Pacific Coastal Airlines is known for being the last company in the world to offer regular flights on a Grumman Goose, of which it owns four. This book is a fictional story of a short flight between Port Hardy and Rivers Inlet with chief pilot Gord Jenkins at the helm.

A lineup of Beavers along the dock in Vancouver.

Chief pilot Gord Jenkins preparing to dock along a pier. He already has the rope ready, which his clients will use to hold the seaplane during unloading and loading.

Restoration of part of the cabin on the Goose C-FUAZ in the workshop of Pacific Coastal Airlines in Port Hardy. Since being built in the 1930s, the aircraft has had all of its parts replaced a minimum of two or three times during servicing. The plane is therefore the same, but none of the parts that make up its whole are original.

A Pratt & Whitney radial engine being inspected on a Beaver in Port Hardy.

The magic of the seaplane, perfectly illustrating the term "flying boat."

The end of the day for a Pacific Coastal Airlines Goose. After three hours of flying time and approximately 170 miles (270 km) traveled, the aircraft is put back in its hangar in Port Hardy. Each of the company's planes has a different drawing on its fin. The one on C-GDDJ represents an Indigenous totem pole.

Flight director Vince Crooks conducts a pre-flight inspection on the Goose C-GDDJ.

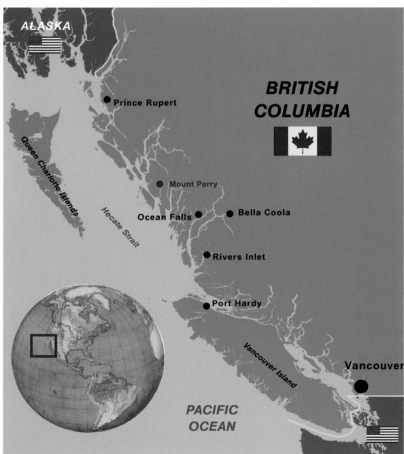

Fresh fruits and vegetables and other supplies ready to be loaded and delivered to a logging camp. The seaplane will stop for only a few minutes before taking off to its next destination. It will complete six such stops during its flight before returning to the dock.

ALASKA

BRITISH
COLUMBIA

Prince Rupert

Queen Charlotte Islands

Hecate Strait

Mount Parry

Ocean Falls • • Bella Coola

Rivers Inlet

Port Hardy

Vancouver Island

Vancouver

PACIFIC
OCEAN

Bibliography

De Goutiere, Justin. *The Pathless Way: Flying the British Columbia Coast*. Vancouver: Douglas & McIntyre, 1968.

Schofield, Jack. *A Pilot's Journey Log: Daryl Smith and Pacific Coastal Airlines*. Mayne Island, BC: CoastDog Press, 2010.

Schofield, Jack. *Flights of a Coast Dog: A Pilot's Log*. Vancouver: Douglas & McIntyre 1999.

Schofield, Jack. *No Numbered Runways: Floatplane Pioneers of the West Coast*. Winlaw BC: Sono Nis Press, 2004.

Stewart, Hilary. *Looking at Indian Art of the Northwest Coast*. Vancouver: Douglas & McIntyre, 1979.

Stewart, Hilary. *Looking at Totem Poles*. Vancouver: Douglas & McIntyre; Seattle: University of Washington Press, 1993.

White, Howard, ed. *Raincoast Chronicles Eleven Up*. Madeira Park BC: Harbour Publishing, 1994.